OH BOTHER!

written by Bronwen Scarffe
illustrated by Juli Kent

BOOKSHELF

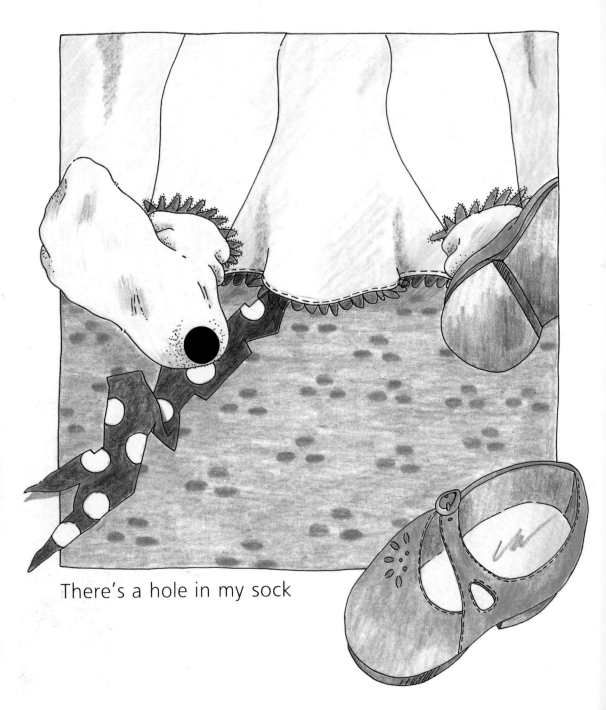

There's a hole in my sock

and a hole in my shoe.

There's a hole in my umbrella
and the rain is coming through.
Oh bother!

There's a hole in my jumper

and a hole in my skirt.

There's a hole in my tooth
and it's starting to hurt.
Oh bother!

There's a hole in my beach ball

and a hole in my kite.

There's a hole in my teddy
where Aussie took a bite.
Oh bother!

There's a hole in my school bag

and a hole in my glove.

There's a hole in my hat
that I really did love.

Oh bother!

There's a hole in my apple

and a hole in my pear.

There's a hole in my pie
and it's dripping everywhere.

Oh bother!